The Far and Wide Travels of Winston Whitten

Story and Illustrations by
Joan Scott Candelmo

Celebrate the little
gifts of life!
Joan Scott Candelmo

The Far and Wide Travels of Winston Whitten

Published by:

Fiddlehead Publishing
Scarborough, Maine 04074

Library of Congress Control Number: 2005928327

ISBN: 0-9667120-7-2

Printed in the USA by

Morris Publishing
3212 East Highway 30 –Kearney, NE 68847
1-800-650-7888

This book is dedicated to my father, E.G. Scott, a Philadelphian, who, like one of the characters in my story, was a masterful writer. He contributed invaluable guidance to the world of medicine while always having a particular fondness for all creatures great and small.

JSC

Covered
bridge

Kancamagus
Highway

Vermont
Farm Fair

WINSTON
WHITTEN'S
TRAVELS
by his own
account...

Lindsay's
home

N
W E
S

Town's End

Boston

Going home →

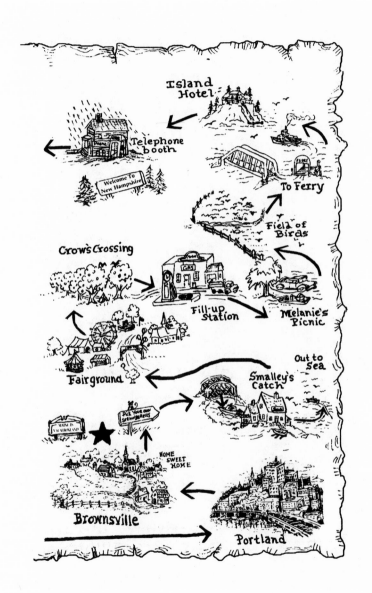

Chapter 1

GETTING THE SCOOP

A Pennsylvanian by birth, Elvin Gerald Scott was simply called E.G. by his many friends and associates. Not liking either his first or middle name, he chose to adopt the pen name, "E. G. Scott." He was a writer, and one who, in earlier times, had been one of the finest newspaper columnists on the East Coast. That was years ago, however . . .

Having recently moved with his wife to the quiet of the southern Maine countryside, he had taken over his town's local paper, *The Brownsville Chronicle.* Interest in the paper had dwindled under the previous

owner, and E.G. Scott had hoped to give it new life when he bought it with some of his retirement money. His dream was to come up with a series of special, on-going, human-interest stories that would run for weeks on end, getting the attention of the town's people, and maybe even other newspapers in New England as well.

He spent many hours at his typewriter, which he had set up in the small deserted barn on his property behind the house. There he would begin to write the stories, and then put the finishing touches on them for final print at his newspaper office in town.

Try as he would, however, whatever ideas he typed out upon the reams of paper at his desk did not seem interesting at all. "I must save this newspaper somehow," he muttered.

Unknown to him, a most unusual mouse had taken up living quarters in E. G.'s writing barn. Fully dressed in a shirt, suit, and tie, leather shoes, and with a smart-looking hat upon his head, he came out of the shadows from the corner of a wooden crate to introduce himself to E. G. Scott.

"They call me W. W., the Star Reporter," he said proudly as he stepped into a beam of sunlight shining across the floor in front of E.G.'s desk, "Otherwise, known by the proper name of Winston Whitten—I got my name from a church hymn book."

"Mercy!" E.G. shouted in complete surprise. "Am I hearing and seeing things, or is this some kind of dream I'm experiencing?"

Winston, who had been used to this type of reaction from people, continued his introduction without concern. "I was originally a member of the Brownsville Congregational Church, living in the church rectory until the cleaning lady discovered me and promptly threw me out on my tail. I never could understand why she thought I could be a threat to the people. The notes that I left for the minister on his desk were often the ideas for many of his sermons. Take for example, the ones I gave him for his, 'All Creatures Great and Small' speech—they were my best!"

"Well, n-now," E.G. Scott stammered as he focused his eyes down on the small animal. "Surely, you must be a creature of my imagination. No one would ever believe that I am here, talking with a mouse!"

"Excuse me, sir, but no one must ever call me a creature or a mouse, for I am who I am, and mighty proud of it—a fine writer and a reporter of news. Along with my partner, I am about to save your newspaper. May I introduce you to Melody Goldfinch, who has the ability to report to you directly from her high-flying position, not only over the town, but great distances beyond?"

Flying down from a high beam over E. G. Scott's desk, a small yellow and brown winged bird gracefully landed next to Winston on the barn floor.

"Most pleased to be of service," she whistled sweetly.

"I don't know what to say or think," E. G. said half to himself and half to the strange couple in front of him.

"Not to worry, sir. If there's a story in town, we'll cover it," Winston stated with assurance.

"Well, I s-suppose . . . ," E. G. stammered again, "I could use all the help that's offered . . . even if it comes from a . . ."

"We'll begin tomorrow," interrupted Winston, "reporting for duty at the first sign of daylight."

"That will be at bird call, 5:30 AM by the clock," chirped Melody.

The next morning, despite his reservations about what he had seen and heard, E. G. Scott awoke before daylight, got dressed, poured himself a cup of coffee, and headed to his writing spot in the barn.

There were the two companions waiting for him with a small notebook propped up on E. G.'s desk, ready to present the day's plans to him.

"Good morning, sir!" they both chimed. "We're all set for you and reporting for duty!"

"Let's get down to business," Winston announced with a degree of authority. "We have a lot of ground to cover!"

"No one will ever believe this," muttered E. G. into his coffee cup.

"My first thought was to cover any stories about the town by myself at *ground level*, so to speak. But, I realized that I have been doing that for quite some time for the church, and figured we needed a wider range to the news."

"That's where I come in," added Melody. "I could cover any breaking reports from a *bird's eye view*, if you will, as far as my wings will take me."

"We both thought she could do a scan of the town as well as other areas each day, and then report back to us what she found. She's ready to take flight at your order, sir."

"Uh, I guess we could see how this would work, if you think you can do it. But, we must not tell anyone, as people might think it was a gimmick or something, coming from a . . ."

"Don't give it another thought, sir," Winston interrupted. "We'll send you whatever we can find without giving away who we are. We can be your secret reporters."

"I'm not sure how I would pay you both . . ." said E. G. Scott, pausing to think how strange it all sounded.

"We're just looking for a place to hang our hats, a comfortable spot to sleep, food and water, et cetera. But, just because we come cheap, sir, doesn't mean that we aren't great reporters," Winston called back as he disappeared across the floorboards.

Chapter 2

FIRST NEWS

For her very first assignment, Melody had returned with the report of what she had seen in the next field. Mr. Flaherty's prized bull had broken through his fence and was heading straight for Mrs. Clampert's beautiful water garden and fishpond.

"Everyone knows how much Mrs. Clampert loves that pond and garden of hers," Melody tweeted with excitement. "Why, just last year she won the Brownsville Garden Club's top award for the Oriental water lilies she raised in that pond. This will be hot news!"

Winston could not wait to start writing it all up from Melody's description. "But first," he said, "I'd better run it by our boss, Mr. Scott!"

When E. G. Scott heard the main part of the story, he scratched his head with his pen. Trying not to discourage his new young reporters, he gently offered his ideas for the kind of story he was hoping to receive from them.

"Let me put it this way," E. G. said softly. "Although I am sure that most of the people in our town would love to know what happened to that bull and Mrs. Clampert's pond, I'm not sure if that kind of news would be as exciting in other towns as well. Perhaps, we could look for something more news-worthy in a broader sense . . . such as the fire that recently broke out in the Woodland Park Range just north of here . . . or, the discovery of water pollution in the Big River and its effect on the salmon industry . . . why the state lobster hauls have been down this year . . . that sort of thing."

"Okay, let's re-group here, Melody," said Winston without a bit of disappointment. "We can do this. You just might need to travel a bit further for that perfect story, Melody. Do you think you can do it?"

"Naturally," answered Melody, not to be deterred. "Have wings – will travel!"

"Then, let's check out a map and see where you might want to go," Winston continued with renewed hopes going on in his mind.

"How about if I simply head north, keep my eyes to the ground, hang out in a few trees and roof tops along the way, and see if I can't come up with a spectacular news item? It may take me at least a day or more to find it, but I'm sure I'll run into something big!"

Chapter 3

NO NEWS

From his hiding place within the wooden crate in the barn, Winston began to pace back and forth while looking at the wind-up watch he had gotten from Mr. Scott to hang up on the wall. Time had gone by slowly since Melody had gone on her northerly flight. By the next nightfall, Winston really began to worry.

Early the following morning, when E. G. Scott came out to his writing spot in the barn, Winston was beside himself with concern. "Something terrible has happened, sir," Winston sputtered. "She should have been back yesterday!"

"What are you talking about . . . er, ah . . . Winston?" E. G. Scott pulled the chair out from his desk, being careful not to tread upon the mouse.

"It's Melody, sir!" Winston replied while walking in circles with his head bent down. "She would never take this long to return!"

"Maybe she's onto something really big and didn't want to leave until she got it all down, Winston."

"I'll give her another day, and if she isn't back by then, I'm going to go look for her," said Winston firmly.

"Look here, Winston. No reporter ever deserts the story no matter how long it takes. The search for the truth and the ideal story is always a long process. Why don't you give her a week, and then begin your search."

"All right, I guess . . . ," answered Winston uneasily. "But, if she's not here by Monday next, I'm on my way!"

"Just how were you planning to get wherever she is – it could be some distance away," replied E. G.

"Well, I was thinking about that when I remembered that your neighbor's son – Duncan, I believe is his name – has one of those gas-powered model cars. Maybe you could ask him if I could borrow it."

"But, how can we tell him about . . . I mean – *you*! Wouldn't that cause a big problem?" E. G. Scott could just imagine what the boy would think when he saw a talking mouse.

"I've discovered that kids are a lot easier with that idea than grownups. They accept what they see and hear, pretty much without question. It is what it is, and that's all there is to that!"

"I hope you're right, Winston, or we might have his parents coming over here to see what kind of nonsense is going on."

"Don't worry, sir. I'll handle it once you can get the boy over here with the model car," Winston replied confidently.

By the end of the week, Winston was anxious to get going on his journey to find Melody. At Winston's request, Mr. Scott met Duncan coming off the school bus down the road and walked over to him.

"Afternoon, Duncan! I wondered if, when you had a chance, you could stop over to my barn. I have a favor to ask of you."

"Sure thing, Mr. Scott. I'll be over as soon as I can get my homework done – my mom's rules, you know! See you then," he called back as he ran off in the direction of his house.

When E. G. Scott and Duncan arrived at the barn, Winston was ready and waiting for them.

"Duncan, nice to meet you! Winston Whitten, here – Star Reporter for the Brownsville Chronicle. We have an important mission to accomplish, and we need your help."

Duncan looked aghast at the small mouse standing upright on Mr. Scott's desk.

"We'd consider it a privilege to use your model car for a very special assignment – that sound okay to you, Duncan?" asked Winston.

Duncan gulped and replied, still in shock, "Yes, I guess so . . . sure!"

"Now, we have to keep this top secret, Duncan, so I want you to swear that no one but you, Mr. Scott, and I will know about this."

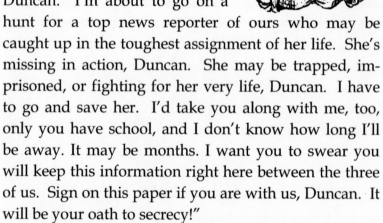

Duncan cleared his throat in rapt attention. "You got it!"

"Now, here's the thing, Duncan. I'm about to go on a hunt for a top news reporter of ours who may be caught up in the toughest assignment of her life. She's missing in action, Duncan. She may be trapped, imprisoned, or fighting for her very life, Duncan. I have to go and save her. I'd take you along with me, too, only you have school, and I don't know how long I'll be away. It may be months. I want you to swear you will keep this information right here between the three of us. Sign on this paper if you are with us, Duncan. It will be your oath to secrecy!"

Without hesitation, while sparks were dancing around in his wide-open eyes, Duncan signed his name. In no time, he was explaining every detail of his model car to Winston—what to do to start it up, how often it would need gas, and how to pull it to a stop by turning the engine off with the switch.

Winston had taken a trial run with Duncan right behind him guiding his every move. However, it was not until the third try that Winston was in full control. He was now ready for his journey to find Melody Goldfinch.

Early the next morning, Winston packed up a few changes of clothes, a little food and water for the trip, along with a pad to keep track of the places he had covered. Saying goodbye to Mr. Scott, who gave him some last words of caution, he got in Duncan's car and started the engine. Although he had no way of knowing Melody's current location, he knew she was headed north. Deciding, therefore, to find a northerly route, he took the first road in that direction to see where that might lead him.

Chapter 4

MOUSE EXCHANGE

Before long, Winston Whitten began to tire from his long journey on the road. He was, after all, as small as a mouse and, for all practical purposes, looked just like a mouse traveling in a small model car over wide and long roads that never seemed to end.

Although he had been gone for only a few days, he was already homesick. He missed the good things that were in his home in the barn—his bed, washing bowl, clean clothes, and his sizable stash of food. He had, however, one overriding thought in his mind and that was to locate his best friend, Melody. Somehow, he would find her—that he knew. But, right now, he was exhausted and hungry.

Looking ahead at a small sign next to the road, he read, "Pick Your Own Straw-berries – Turn Right Here." That sounded like a perfect meal to Winston, so he made a right turn onto the bumpy dirt road. Just as he approached the farm gates at the end of the road, a field mouse scurried across the fence in front of him.

"Hold on a minute, if you would, sir," called Winston Whitten. "I noticed your sign down the road."

"What sign?" asked the field mouse, pausing to give Winston a good looking over. Never before had he seen a mouse in elegant attire such as Winston Whitten was wearing. *Must be one of those big town mice*, thought the field mouse to himself.

"You know, the sign about the strawberries," replied Winston.

"Oh, *that* sign! No strawberries in the farmer's field this early. You'll have to wait until June," answered the field mouse.

Winston sighed, "Well, whoever this farmer is, he surely shouldn't be leaving his sign up all year to trick folks, especially one as hungry as I am!"

"If it's food you want, I'll be glad to share some of mine. Park that machine of yours next to the gate, and follow me through the tall grass," said the field mouse.

"Just a little further ahead," the trail blazer called back to Winston.

He was face-up to the sides of a big red barn when he caught up to his new friend. A small hole gnawed into the bottom of one of the barn's boards turned out to be a mouse-sized entry, and they both scurried through the opening.

Winston looked around inside of the milking barn in amazement. He had never before seen such a large barn with so many stalls. The sweet smell of grasses permeated this room just as it had done in the field. He followed the field mouse around some wooden dividers.

"Watch out!" called the field mouse. "The cows in those stalls have been known to tromp on a few of us by accident."

Winston couldn't believe what he saw. "A cow is a mighty big creature, and not something I'd care to run into," he said aloud. He remembered seeing a

picture of one on the side of a milk bottle once, but had no idea that they could be as large as a milk truck!

As they both rounded the food trough, there, under the hay, was a comfortable-looking nest.

"Welcome to our home," said the field mouse,

while four sets of bright beady eyes peered out at Winston from the down-filled interior.

After introductions to his family, the field mouse pulled out some dried corn kernels and a mushroom cap filled with water.

Winston had become used to Mr. Scott's more elegant food offerings recently, but he was pleased to be accepted at the mouse family's meal table.

"You may sleep here tonight, if you'd like," offered the field mouse's wife. "But, we have to be careful of the black snake who roams around the barn in the early morning hours. My uncle was swallowed whole last week by that snake!"

Winston thanked them kindly, but decided that he had a few hours of daylight left in which to travel, and he had better be off down the road again.

Much relieved to be back in his car and under his own power of destiny, Winston waved good-by, and headed in the direction of the main road, traveling north once again.

Chapter 5

THE OPEN SEA

Going across a large span-bridge, Winston had not noticed how fast he had been driving when, all too late, his car fell through a hole in one of the bridge planks, heading for the river below.

A fisherman had been steering his boat homeward from the open sea and was under the bridge at the exact moment that Winston was falling. Luckily, Winston and his car landed into a pile of the fisherman's nets inside the stern of the boat.

Despite the fishy odor, Winston decided that he had better get out of his car and survey the situation. Try as he might, he could not get either door open, realizing that his car had become entwined in the net.

As the boat pulled up to its moorings, and the captain climbed out of the boat to tie it to the dock, Winston knew that it was too late to call out for help. That night, he would be rocked to sleep by the gentle movement of the boat upon the water's edge.

He pulled his jacket over his body and stretched out across the car's seat as best as possible. He dreamed he was being saved by his dear friend, Melody, who was flying him back to his home in Brownsville.

The next morning before sunrise, Winston awoke to the roar of the boat's engine. The fisherman was heading out to sea again for his daily haul of fish. Winston had never been fishing out in the ocean before, and, although he could not see out beyond his trapped car, he could smell the salt air and hear the sea gulls flying above him.

Suddenly, he was being propelled out of the boat stuck inside the netting, as the fisherman cast it overboard. Winston was headed for the ocean waves!

Just as he was saying a little prayer to bless Mr. Scott, Melody, and Duncan, that they might remember him after he was gone, one of the seagulls swooped down and grabbed Winston's car out of the net with her long claws. Winston and his car went flying upward and over the ocean before the seagull came to land on the shore nearby.

"I thought you were a shiny fresh fish," said the seagull, peeping at Winston through the car window.

"What a disappointment!"

Winston, wondering if seagulls ever ate objects his size, politely addressed the seagull from inside his car. "I' m very grateful to you for saving my life."

"Well, it wasn't quite what I had in mind," muttered the seagull curtly.

"And," continued Winston, "I would be even more grateful if you would place my car onto to some flat land so that I could be on my way."

"What would you do for me if I did?" coaxed the seagull.

"If you would follow my car, I am sure that I could find some fresh fish along the way," said Winston, not knowing how he was going to fulfill this promise.

"Very well," said the gull. "I shall carry you

inland until I find the nearest road."

As luck would have it, the road led immediately to a small fish market named Smalley's Catch.

Winston pulled up to the entrance. Meanwhile, the seagull perched nearby to keep a watchful eye on Winston's movements.

Cautiously, Winston got out of the car and went inside the store.

The shop owner, Mr. Smalley, himself, was behind the counter. "How can I help you?" he asked, smiling down at Winston.

That was just what Winston wanted to hear! He pulled himself up and onto a pickling barrel and began to tell his story about how he had been saved by a seagull from the open sea. He explained the promise he had made to the seagull for some fresh fish.

Mr. Smalley scratched his grizzly beard, allowing a large cloud of smoke to leave his pipe and circle his head.

"Let me see," he said with some hesitation. "I cannot give away my good fish. But, I do have some fish parts out back in the trash buckets that your friend is welcome to have."

"I can't thank you enough," coughed Winston from under the smoky cloud. Then, he dashed out of Mr. Smalley's market waving the seagull to the back of the building.

From the rearview window of his car, Winston watched the hungry gull eagerly gulp down the catch. Then, he quickly sped off down the road to wherever it would take him, leaving the gull behind.

Chapter 6

COME JOIN THE PARADE

In the distance, Winston thought that he was seeing his new friend, Duncan. The further he drove down the road, he could see that it was a boy trying to get a red balloon down from the nearby tree branches.

"Wow, swell car!" cried the boy. Winston stepped out of the car to see the boy's surprised expression.

"How did you do that?" asked the boy in amazement.

"Do *what*?" Winston asked back.

"Shrink yourself into mouse-size so you could drive that thing," said the boy.

"This *is* my natural size," said Winston stiffly.

"Have you ever been in a circus before?" asked the boy.

"I haven't had the pleasure," answered Winston in a gruff tone.

"Well, hey, gee whiz, you've got to be in our parade!" said the boy, bopping his balloon with his fist.

"What parade?"

Leaning over Winston and picking up his car to

examine it, the boy continued his conversation. "Our town's centennial parade—*that's* what parade."

Winston Whitten began to be interested. "Tell me about it," he said as he sat himself down on the side of the road.

"There's gonna' be a band and everything! And, my mom says they're selling hot dogs, soda pop, popcorn balls, and all kinds of pies! Hey, if you were in our parade, I'd bet you'd win a prize!"

Winston was beginning to get rather hungry at the thought of homemade pies and popcorn balls. *Maybe it wouldn't be such a bad idea to see what this parade is all about after all.*

"Hurry up!" cried the boy. "We've gotta' get you to meet the mayor. He'll get you in the parade!"

So, Winston climbed back into his car and followed the boy with the balloon into the center of town.

 Everyone was bustling about setting up booths, checking out the costumes for the parade, tuning instruments for the band, and putting the final ties on the banners all over town.

Groups of people had gathered around a platform in the middle of the town park and were making a fuss over a rather stout gentleman in a top hat and with a carnation in his suit lapel.

"Mr. Mayor!" called the boy from across the lawn. "Have I got something terrific to show you!" He gave Winston's car a quick push with his foot, landing it smack up against the stout man's shiny black shoes.

"What have we here?" the mayor asked, somewhat aghast.

Everyone peered down at Winston as he opened his car door, stepped out, and tipped his hat to the mayor.

"W. W., Star Reporter from The Brownsville Chronicle, sir," Winston said as elegantly as possible.

"Well, I'll be!" exclaimed the mayor. "This belong to you, boy?"

"No, sir," the boy grinned with excitement, "but,

I sure would like to enter him in our parade!"

Down Main Street came the floats and the band, and ahead of the band came the town's mayor riding in a white limousine decorated with American flags. But, right at the very front of the parade was Winston Whitten in his car, atop a moving float festooned with red, white, and blue streamers and balloons.

The boy and several of his friends, pulling the float with pride, strode down the street, as the crowd clapped and shouted, "Hooray!"

Winston's float won first

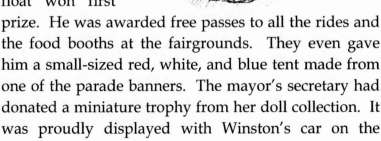

prize. He was awarded free passes to all the rides and the food booths at the fairgrounds. They even gave him a small-sized red, white, and blue tent made from one of the parade banners. The mayor's secretary had donated a miniature trophy from her doll collection. It was proudly displayed with Winston's car on the platform for all to see.

After a lengthy speech from the mayor and a brief history of the town that was given by the pastor of the Trinity Church, the crowd moved to the fairgrounds. The boy, feeling like the ultimate winner, carried Winston around in his pocket as if he were a personal trophy.

Visiting the food booths, Winston had some licks of Gunther's hand-churned ice cream, a tiny slice of Lois Temple's fresh cherry pie, two bites from a popcorn ball, and several slurps of Cain's root beer soda pop.

Just when Winston was beginning to feel quite overstuffed, the boy took him on the merry-go-round.

When the carousel finally came to a stop, a queasy Winston made a dash for a nearby table with the boy running after him.

Unfortunately, as Winston pulled himself up the side of the tablecloth to the top of the table, the boy reached out for him, knocking Winston into the middle of May Jenner's banana cream pie! Miss Jenner grabbed the boy by the ear, scolding him with harsh words.

Winston saw this as his chance to get away, and, although sticky with banana cream, managed to get back to his parked car.

Snatching a towel he had in his knapsack, he wiped himself off as best as possible. Then, he started his car engine, bumped down the steps of the mayor's platform, and headed for the open road.

Leaving the small town, Winston stopped for a quick sponge bath in a nearby creek, breathed a sigh of relief, and began to feel more like himself again.

Chapter 7

CROWS' CROSSING

It had been a long day, and Winston was extremely tired. Driving along down the road, he began looking for a comfortable spot to set up his new tent for a night's rest. A shady grove of apple trees looked like a good area in which to settle, so he drove his car off the side of the road and parked under the first tree.

Wearily, he put up his tent and crawled inside. Tomorrow, he would write a letter to Mr. Scott back in

Brownsville, letting him know of his latest adventures.
He always missed his home most at nighttime.

The next morning, Winston awoke to some loud
squawking coming from
two crows on the
branches above his tent.

"Now that
you've so rudely
awakened me,"
grumbled Winston,
rubbing his eyes, "Do
you happen to know
what part of the country
we are in at present?"

"We just got here
this morning, ourselves,
after a long flight," said
the larger crow.

"Haven't had
much time to check out
the territory," said the other.

Instantly thinking about his own feathered
friend, Melody, Winston asked, "By any chance, have
you seen a small brown bird with a yellow breast in
your travels?"

"We've seen quite a few small birds flying north
above us," pondered one of the crows. "Were you
looking for someone in particular?"

"Yes," said Winston. "I'm looking for a bird
named Melody. She comes from Brownsville where

wheat fields are vast and thistle grows deep, and she loves to sing. Oh, yes—she's also a newspaper reporter on an important assignment."

"She could be with that flock we saw yesterday headed in that direction," said the larger crow pointing with his wing.

"It's worth a try," said Winston, as he began to pack up his belongings and to carry them to his car.

"Good luck!" *cawed* the two crows in unison, as they headed skyward over the apple orchard.

Chapter 8

CONTINUING NORTH

Winston remembered that he had promised himself that he would get a letter off to Mr. Scott along the way. Before going on the road again, he reached for his reporter's notepad and put some of his news in writing:

Dear Mr. Scott,

After a series of adventures, which would make up an entire book, I still have not found Melody. The weather has been pleasant, however. Despite a few mishaps along the way, I am in relatively fine shape.

He closed with a brief description of his last two days, then signed,

Your Star Reporter,
Winston Whitten

P.S Please tell Duncan his car is working great!

He hoped that his comment about the model car would please Duncan. Then, affixing a stamp to the envelope that he kept folded in his pocket for such an occasion, he started up the engine of his car.

"Getting a little low on fuel," he noted aloud to himself. "I'd better find a nearby town."

Two short hills later, Winston saw the beginnings of a town beyond him, complete with a gas station and a post office directly ahead.

"What good fortune," he said, coming up and over the last hill.

Just as he was pulling up to the pump, a rattling red truck almost ran over him, with its breaks squealing.

"So sorry about that," said the tall thin man, stepping down from his truck. "I'm not seeing things so well these days."

Winston brushed the dust off his sleeves and stood well out of the man's shadow.

"Farmer Jim, they call me. I came for some gas for 'ole Sally here, but it looks as though the attendant has closed the station for the day."

"Winston Whitten, here to do the same," said Winston, wondering what he was going to do now.

"Well," said Farmer Jim, "guess we won't be able to get anything here. I still have enough gas to get me to the station on the other side of town. Why don't we put you and your motor car in the back of my truck, and I'll give you a hitch there?"

"Awfully kind of you," smiled Winston. "And, while we're at it, could we stop by that post office to mail my letter?"

"Mighty small letter," grinned the man, "but, I guess it will get where it's goin' just as well as any."

Soon, they were off down the road with Winston in tow.

The town itself was quite big, with many large mill factories, steeple churches, and dry goods stores along the main streets. Although it was not to be compared to his beloved Brownsville, it seemed to have quite a hub of activity within its center. They passed a school with a large park nearby that was filled with children playing and running.

Crossing over a railroad track, Winston noticed that the landscape was thinning out, and a number of comfortable-looking houses dotted the landscape.

With a wide turn of the truck that almost sent Winston and his car off the back, Farmer Jim pulled into a busy gasoline station. There were several trucks waiting for their turns at the pump, as well as a spanking new convertible, as their truck joined the line.

"Gas for two!" shouted Farmer Jim, when it was their turn. Even though the attendant looked a bit perplexed, he managed to find a way to get some fuel into Winston's small car.

"Where are you headed?" the nice-looking young woman in the convertible called over to Winston.

"North," said Winston.

"Perhaps, I could save you some time on the road," she said, looking down at the size of Winston's car. "I'm headed to Grand Isle to visit my aunt for the next few weeks. You could join me in the front seat for the trip."

"Grand Isle, you say?" Winston asked nervously. "Is that north of here?"

"You couldn't get much further north unless you wanted to go into Canada," laughed the young woman. "By the way, my name is Melanie," she said lifting Winston and his car to the seat beside her.

What a coincidence, thought Winston. *I'm looking for someone with almost the same name.* "Thank you for the invitation, Melanie. My name is Winston Whitten."

"I'm pleased to have your company, Winston," smiled Melanie.

After thanking Farmer Jim for all of his help, he waved good-by, and got himself comfortable next to his lovely new companion.

Stopping off to share Melanie's picnic lunch,

Winston realized that he had not even had breakfast that day. Her cheese and crackers hit the spot, as did her very own chocolate brownies with nuts on top.

Chatting cheerfully with Melanie reminded him of the last time he had gone to a church picnic. Being with her was quite enjoyable, and, he noted, she was also very pretty.

As they neared the coastline, Winston could feel the difference in the air. The cool breeze flowing through the open convertible had the smell of pine trees and the ocean brine all in one. It was intoxicating. Winston could have traveled this way forever, but his mission to find Melody suddenly came to mind, and he began to look for open fields and pastures.

"I guess I had better think of going off on my own again," uttered Winston with a sigh.

"Any particular destination?" asked Melanie.

"Not really," answered Winston, "but I'm looking for my friend who may have flown this way."

"By plane?" asked Melanie.

"No, by wing. She's a bird, and she loves thistle fields."

"Perhaps those fields over there in the valley might be a possibility," said Melanie. "There seems to be lots of thistle in them."

Somehow, Winston felt that Melanie had some special connection to his friend, Melody. And, if she thought those fields might be the right place, that is where he would go.

"It's been wonderful," said Melanie, as she patted Winston's head with her delicate finger.

"For me, too," said Winston wistfully. "I can't thank you enough."

Chapter 9

FIELD OF BIRDS

Heading onto a winding wagon trail through the field before him, Winston almost popped a tire on his car. But, he couldn't help feeling that this might be the perfect place in which a flock of birds might stop for a rest. Certainly, the fields were abloom with thistle and wild bush berries, a bird's food of choice.

Stopping his car to look through the wide fields,

Winston could hardly believe his eyes! There was a flurry of small birds just beyond him! Could it be that he really might find Melody in this very spot?

Excitement could scarcely keep him from running into the open field, but he knew that the sudden movement might frighten the birds away. So, he tried to contain himself and sat there patiently.

A small bird with a yellow tinge landed on a thistle plant next to him. "Melody!" he cried.

"Goodness, you startled me!" said the bird. "My name is Ginny. Who is it you called for?"

"My name is Winston Whitten, and I have come a long way hoping to find my friend, Melody," said a disappointed Winston.

"I can see by your face that you are most anxious to find her, and, as your luck would have it, I happen to know a Melody," said the bird. "She hooked up with our flock about three days ago."

"Where is she? I must see her!" cried Winston, afraid to believe that this moment was real.

"I have to tell you that we have been very worried about her," said the bird. "When we stopped here yesterday, she got injured by a Cooper's hawk while trying to divert the hawk from catching a mouse she thought she knew," continued the bird. "She has been resting in the grasses. We all have been afraid to leave her behind, but her wing has been hurt, and she can not fly for awhile."

Winston almost flew from the rock in search of her. "Melody! Melody!" he cried.

"Over here! Could that be you, Winston, really *you*?" cried Melody, hunched down in the tall field grass.

Winston gave her a careful hug so as not to touch the injured wing. "It's going to be all right, Melody! I'm here and I can take care of you! Look over there—I even have my own car!"

Melody could not have been happier than to see her friend again. As they sat together, Melody explained why she had been gone for so long. She was following a run-away bear from the traveling Bingham Brothers Circus and stayed with the story until the bear was rescued. Then, as she was about to report back to Brownsville, she came across a flock of her own kind going north. They were headed to a grand reunion of over a thousand birds in the highlands. She decided to join them for a while, when the accident occurred in the field with the hawk. Then, Winston shared with her all about his own adventures leading up to his fortune in finding her at last.

"Well, we *are* a pair, aren't we, Winston?" laughed Melody.

"And, now," said Winston, "we've got to get you to my car so you'll be safe in my care."

"Where are we going, Winston?" worried Melody.

"I was planning to take you back to Brownsville with me so you could rest up and regain your health," replied Winston.

"But, what about the stories for the newspaper?" cried Melody.

"A few days of rest will do wonders for you—you'll see," said one of the birds.

"Let's build her a stretcher to get her to my car," suggested Winston.

In a matter of minutes, the other birds and Winston had assembled two pieces of bark sewn together with vines, and covered them with soft moss. Winston gently helped Melody onto the stretcher, and one of the birds pulled the ends of the vines over her, tying her in securely.

"I don't know what all the fuss is about," said
Melody. "I've only injured my wing. I can still hop!"

"Easy does it!" ordered Winston, as four birds
picked up the edges of the stretcher in their beaks and
lifted her up through the grasses to Winston's car.

Winston opened the door to the passenger side
of the car with a grand gesture.
"This way, M'lady!"

The other birds
carefully tucked Melody
into the front seat and
chirped their good-
byes.

"Thank you,
Winston," said Melody,
leaning over to give him a
soft peck with her bill.

"You're an angel sent from heaven!"

Chapter 10

ISLAND HOTEL VACATION

"We really should have a map to see where we're going, Winston," said Melody. "When I could fly, I could easily see ahead for miles, and everything looked like a map below me."

"Not to worry," responded Winston with a smile—even though he, himself, was beginning to do just that. But, he wanted to put Melody's mind at ease.

A few minutes later, Winston saw a road sign that read, "Bridge and Ferry Up Ahead."

"I wonder if you would like to take the ferry across, instead of using the bridge," suggested Winston, remembering his traumatic fall from an earlier bridge, which he had tried to cross in his little car.

"It might be fun," answered Melody.

As the two friends drove down to the pier, they caused quite a spectacle among all the tourists boarding the ferryboat.

The boat's attendant let Winston's car on first to avoid being trampled by the larger autos. Winston and Melody thought that they were being treated like special guests.

As the ferry sailed off, it seemed to Melody that it was heading out to sea. A half an hour later, the ferry arrived at its destination.

"All out for your island vacation!" called a young man with an official-looking cap on his head.

"What island?" cried Winston, looking nervously at Melody.

All the people began departing from the ferry carrying suitcases and trunks up the hill from the dock.

"Are you staying at the Island Hotel, too?" asked the pleasant woman standing next to them.

"Why not?" smiled Melody, feeling newly refreshed with the clean ocean air. "The rest will, no doubt, do us both some good."

Winston and
Melody became the
preferred guests of the
hotel. Every evening
after supper in the
dining room, Winston
and Melody would be
the entertainment for
the rest of the guests.
Winston would climb
upon the piano and
hop about the keys,

playing tunes that he had practiced on the piano in the Brownsville Church when it had been closed up for the night. And, Melody became known as the best whistler ever, as she sang to Winston's music.

Because of their remarkable talents, not only did Winston and Melody get to have their own room at the hotel, but, they received all their meals *on the house*, as well. They had become very friendly with the hotel's cook, who made special blueberry pancakes and blueberry muffins just the right size for them every morning. And, although the cook was most well known for her marvelous clam chowders and baked, stuffed lobsters, for Winston and Melody, she always had corn muffins fresh from the oven, with raspberry preserves to put on top.

In the daytime, when Winston and Melody were not busy entertaining the guests, they would sun

themselves on the rocks by the shore and count the starfish along the beach. Winston collected a few eye-catching seashells for himself and a small crab shell

for his new friend, Duncan. For Mr. Scott, he found a nautical button in the sand, *probably lost from some sea captain's jacket*, figured Winston.

Melody contented herself by basking in the sun, feeling better each day of her wonderful vacation.

On the fourth evening of their stay at the hotel, and right in the middle of Melody and Winston's marvelous concert, one of the guests let out a loud scream.

"Bats!" yelled the young boy from the back of the room. With that announcement, everyone began running in all directions in and out of the

room, while holding onto the tops of their heads in a panic.

Winston and Melody could not believe how

frightened everyone was. Winston had seen bats before in Mr. Scott's barn, and they seemed to look like mice with wings to him. Melody, equally unconcerned, tried to assure the people that anything that small with wings couldn't be all that bad.

The hotel manager kept muttering, "I can't imagine how they got onto this island! I must do something to get rid of them, or my guests will want to leave the hotel!"

Winston thought of a plan to help the hotel manager. He suggested that the people return to their rooms, while he and Melody devise a way to round up the bats and get them into a lobster trap for safe keeping. Winston had the cook find her best jar of apricot jelly and pour some of it into bowls for inside the lobster trap.

Winston and Melody waited, not moving an inch until the nighttime, when the bats began their flight. Winston remembered reading that bats had a particular fondness for apricot nectar. Sure enough, they flew into the lobster trap where they became caged.

Since Winston and Melody thought that it was about time to start getting back to their travels, they agreed to make sure that the bats could return on the

ferry with them. Then, Winston would release them into the fields once the ferry got back to the mainland.

Everyone thought that Melody and Winston were the best part of their vacation on the island. How brave they were, too! The hotel manager very proudly told them both that they had an open invitation to come back to his hotel anytime that they wanted to, and at absolutely no cost, *of course*!

Chapter 11

THE PHONE CALL

R ain showers moved over the sky just as Winston
and Melody seemed to be making some headway
on their travels.

"We'd better pull over until this downpour is
over," Winston counseled Melody. "I won't be able to
see much of the road with all of these raindrops covering my view."

Winston
pulled up along-
side of a small
roadside variety
store. Maneuver-
ing around the
base of a water-
gushing rain-
spout, he parked
his car
underneath the
overhang of a tin
roof. Looking
through the rain-

spotted windows, Winston could see that the roof belonged to an outside phone booth.

Melody and Winston waited out the rain, chatting about where they should go next in search of some breaking news.

The shower passed almost as quickly as it had begun, and the sun appeared from behind a cloud.

"Back on the road!" cried Winston. But, Melody, who was feeling a bit hungry, pleaded with Winston to make a brief survey of the area for something to eat before going on.

"I suppose that isn't a bad idea," said Winston, opening the car door.

As he walked a few steps from where he had parked, he noticed a shiny paper wrapper on the ground. Although wet from the rain, the wrapper had not been opened, and the crackers were dry and crispy.

"Perfect," smiled Melody. "They even have sesame seeds on top!"

Winston, who was not all that hungry, decided

to stroll around while Melody ate. He came upon another shiny object which was sticking out of a puddle near the phone booth.

"Heavens!" he cried. "I think I've found a treasure!"

As he tugged at the round object, he discovered that it was a coin.

"My goodness!" he shouted. "Someone must have dropped this when they used the phone!" Suddenly, the thought ran through his mind that, perhaps, he could use the coin to call Mr. Scott back in Brownsville!

He had not contacted him since the day he left some time ago. It would be a good idea to do it now.

"But, how will you reach the phone?" asked Melody, knowing that she would not be able to help him because of her wounded wing.

"I'll back up the car into the phone booth, climb on top of the car roof, then jimmy up the phone cord," answered Winston excitedly.

"How will you get the coin up there?" asked Melody, always one to notice the details.

"Perhaps, I could have you help me tie the coin to my back. Then, when I get to the top of the phone machine, I could untie it and lower it into the money slot."

It sounded good in the planning stage, but once Winston had gotten up to the top, somehow managing to lower the coin into the slot, he had not realized the difficulty of the rest of the task.

"You have to dial the operator," called Melody from inside the car.

Winston lowered himself as carefully as possible to the clip on the phone dial where "O" for operator fortunately was located.

Hanging onto the clip with his hands, he began propelling the dial in a circular motion. Exhausted as he was, he finally completed the 325 degree turn of the dial. Then, the dial spun backwards, catching Winston on the way. Winston was spun back onto the ground.

From the receiver, a loud voice called, "Your number, ple-ase!"

Winston brushed himself off and began his climb back up the cord once more.

Again, the voice from the phone seemed to shout, "Hallo, hallo—this is your operator! What *number* did you want?"

Winston barely made it to the top of the receiver cord, and then swung himself on the cord like a clock pendulum, shouting with all his strength into the voice box as he swung in front of it.

"2 – 0 – 7, 5 – 8 – 0 – 1 - 1 – 1 – 2," called Winston.

"Could you repeat that?" called the operator loudly. "I could barely hear you!"

Once again, Winston swung himself across, but this time, he grabbed a hold of the horn of the voice box. After shouting the number over several times, the operator finally got through to Brownsville.

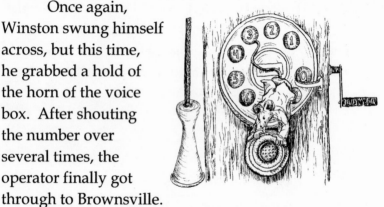

"Will you accept a long-distance call from a Winston Whitten?" the operator asked a very surprised Mrs. Scott.

"*Who?*" asked a perplexed Mrs. Scott.

"Winston Whitten, the Star Reporter for the Brownsville Chronicle, m'am," squeaked Winston as loudly as possible. "Could I please speak to Mr. Scott?"

"Well, yes. I'll get him. Just a moment, please." Winston could hear her turn from the phone to call out to her husband, "Dear, come quickly! It's a reporter for the paper! Says his name is Whitten."

"I'm so relieved to hear from you, Winston!" E. G. Scott said into the phone.

Taking his role as a reporter seriously, Winston went straight to the facts and told his boss briefly about his journey and how he finally found Melody.

"Where are you now, Winston?" Mr. Scott asked.

"I'm not sure, but we can see lots of mountains beyond the town we're in." After a long pause, Winston added, "I'm sorry to tell you this, sir, but we only have a few stories that may or may not be worthy of reporting."

"Don't worry, Winston," replied Mr. Scott. "The important thing is that you both are safe."

"If you could call what has happened to us along the way *safe!*" cried Winston.

"What do you mean, Winston?" asked a worried Mr. Scott.

"Well, for starters, I fell through a bridge and landed on a boat going out to the ocean before almost being eaten alive by a seagull; then Melody got injured by a hawk just as I was about to find her, and we both were taken to an island by mistake; and next, we had to get rid of some bats in a hotel . . ." puffed Winston, almost out of breath.

"Wait a minute!" cried Mr. Scott. "I suddenly have a fabulous idea! *You two* will be the story!"

"What?"

"Listen to me, Winston! Just think of it—an honest-to-goodness writing mouse and bird, reporting their adventures across the country! The public will go wild! Why didn't I think of this before? What about it, Winston?" asked an excited Mr. Scott.

"I suppose I could check with Melody to see what she thinks about it, sir. Do you actually believe that people will take to the idea?" asked Winston with hesitation.

"It could make you both famous all over the country . . . the world even! Wait until I tell Mrs. Scott about this! I've been wanting to tell her about you and Melody all along!" Mr. Scott could hardly contain himself with the thought of it all.

After quickly relaying Mr. Scott's ideas to Melody, Winston continued on the phone, "Melody likes your plan, sir. I guess we both have agreed to it. As a matter of fact, now that I think more about it, it will be great!" replied Winston, getting caught up in the excitement. "We're set to continue our journey, Mr. Scott!"

"Now, do take care of each other and come back safely," cautioned E. G. Scott. He then went on to suggest that Winston might find a map at the nearby store, or ask someone for directions so they would know where they were going.

Winston ended the call promising that he would, and that he also would do his best to get back to him somehow as they traveled along the way.

Winston felt exhilarated with the new proposal and pleased with himself that he had been able to make that call.

"Don't forget that you're going to have to climb back down that phone cord again. Be careful!" called Melody, interrupting his dreamy state.

One more struggle maneuvering over the phone box and Winston climbed down the cord, while deeply absorbed in his thoughts of their new role for the newspaper and the extended journey they would plan. He and Melody had a long road ahead of them, hopefully with many new adventures awaiting them before they returned home.

Chapter 12

TRAIL BLAZING

Not forgetting his promise to Mr. Scott, Winston stopped in the variety store to ask for a map.

"Don't sell them here," said the storekeeper. "Not much call for them in these parts," he continued.

"Where exactly *are* these parts, if you please?" Winston asked as politely as possible.

"Not far from the Kancamagus Highway," the

shopkeeper replied.

"If you don't mind telling me, sir, what is the Kancamagus Highway?" Winston dared to ask.

"It's the best place of beauty we've got around here."   The shopkeeper added, "Also brings people from away."

"The tourists, you mean?" Winston guessed.

"Yep, it's what keeps us goin' all year 'round . . . . the fall foliage, the winter skiin', the spring hikin', the summer campin'. . . ." the shopkeeper went on.

"How do I get there?" asked Winston, resorting to *Plan B—Ask for Directions.*

"Up the road a piece," he answered, waving his arm in a general direction. "You can't miss it," he said, as Winston, somewhat perplexed and with shoulders slumped, walked out of the store mumbling, "Thank you."

Melody was getting sleepy, as birds do when the sun begins to set over the horizon. Winston, also tired from all the traveling, started looking for a good place to rest for the night.

As they were driving up a winding mountain road, a small group of people with hiking boots, walking sticks, and back packs crossed in front of them.

Winston called out from his car window, "Pardon me, but is there a safe place to pitch a tent around here?" "Certainly," replied one of the hikers. "We've just come off the Appalachian Trail where there are plenty of tenting areas. We were stopping off to pick up a few supplies, but we'd be glad to point you in the

right direction."

Not only did they find a spot to put up the tent, but the hikers also returned to help them build a small campfire nearby to keep them warm during the cool night air of the mountain range.

As Melody and Winston settled down in their comfortable tent together, they looked out through the tent opening at the beautiful scene of the night. The dark mountains that were silhouetted across the violet sky became the perfect backdrop for the sparkling lights of the stars above and the crackling coals of their campfire. Sleep came easily for them both.

Chapter 13

OFF TO THE FAIR

The next morning, the same friendly group of hikers checked back with Winston and Melody to make sure that they were all right. The woman hiker had collected a handful of bushberries for their breakfast.  Another hiker taught Winston how to safely put out a campfire. He led him to a nearby stream, and helped him collect enough water to soak the remaining coals and to bury them once they were cold.

Melody did her best with her good wing to sweep the area where the tent had been and place pine needles over the ground to restore it to its natural appearance. Once everything was taken care of, Winston and Melody checked their campsite once again and climbed into the car certain that they left the area in safe order as the hikers had taught them. They felt like true trailblazers.

On the road again, they drove around the winding mountain and discovered the beauty of the Kancamagus Highway, with all of the surrounding trees, streams, and vistas along the way.

Everywhere they looked, there was something to see. At one point, they caught sight of some white-tailed deer, and further along, a moose

 among the trees. Finally, on the way down the other side of the mountain, they came to a covered bridge stretched out over a running river.

"Oh, Bother!" mumbled Winston, not wanting to use the bridge, but attempting to keep his fear to himself. He was just about determined to steer straight ahead and drive forward, when a horse and wagon filled with hay pulled up behind them.

"Only room on the bridge for one of us at a time," called down the driver, "but, if you want to have a ride on my wagon, we can go over it together."

"That would be mighty fine with us," said Winston, breathing a sigh of relief.

With some help from the driver, who lifted them up to the back of the wagon with his pitchfork, they had crossed the darkened bridge in no time.

"I'm headed to the Vermont Fairgrounds up beyond. I'd be glad to take you along if you are going that way, too," the driver called back.

Winston looked at Melody, and Melody shrugged her good shoulder. "Sure, why not?" said Winston. "We'd be most grateful."

Chapter 14

A CHANCE ENCOUNTER

When they arrived at the fairgrounds, there were more farm animals than either Melody or Winston had ever seen. The stocks were filled with prize cattle, sheep, and pigs.

Farm families proudly brushed and groomed their own special entries for the competitions. Blue

ribbons were to be awarded to the best of the breeds. But, a red ribbon or a yellow ribbon was quite exciting to receive as well. The big tents had booths and booths of food, tables displaying crafts made by the women and the children, and exhibits of the latest farm equipment and best-buy seeds.

Winston and Melody particularly liked the area that held the baby farm animals. Along with the piglets and the newly born lambs, there were chicks and young ducklings.

Winston hopped up on a milking stool to get a better view of a small brown and white pony in the next fenced-in area, when he could not believe what he saw riding on top . . . it was a young girl no bigger than Winston, himself!

"Well, I'll be!" cried Winston with astonishment. "Do you see her, Melody? She's our size! I'm going to have to go over and introduce myself. Wait here for me a moment."

As soon as the young rider had dismounted from her pony using a specially made foot ladder, Winston quietly walked over to her from the backside, going wide around the pony's legs.

"Oh, my goodness! You really startled me!" she said turning around to face Winston. "I'm Lindsay White from Town's End, Massachusetts. And, who might you be?"

"I'm Winston Whitten, Star Reporter for the Brownsville Chronicle in Maine," answered Winston with a slight bow.

"I'm delighted to meet you," said Lindsay with a smile. "I've never had the opportunity to meet anyone of my height before—I'm usually the odd one out. By the way, what brings you here to the fair-grounds?"

"My partner and I have been covering the news over these parts as we travel along, collecting stories for our boss, Mr. E. G. Scott and his newspaper. And, what, may I ask, are you doing here?" Winston asked while attempting to take notes on his writing pad as a true reporter would.

"My father always brings me to the Vermont Fairgrounds each year so that I can enter my pony in the exhibition. He has received quite a few ribbons over the years, you know."

Winston led Lindsay over to the fence to intro-duce her to Melody, and then explained to her how he had recently found Melody when she became lost on a mission for the newspaper. Melody was amazed to see a young girl the same size as she and Winston. After they had gotten through all the shared stories, Lindsay tied her pony up to the fence, and the three of them began walking towards the fair together.

Lindsay introduced them to her parents who took them over to the food tent and treated them to a fine lunch of farm-fresh cheese, home-baked bread, pure cow's milk, and Mrs. White's own Apple Brown Betty for dessert.

The more they all continued to chat together, Lindsay thought that it would be a wonderful idea for them to come back home with her and stay awhile at Town's End.

"That certainly would be nice of you, provided," said Winston, "that you will visit us in Brownsville at some time."

"That would be great!" replied Lindsay.

And so it was arranged that, after the fair, Winston and Melody would accompany Lindsay and her parents to Town's End. This, of course, would save Winston and Melody a lot of time in traveling, cutting their trip back to Maine by many days of road driving. In the meantime, still nibbling on bits of dessert, they got to watch Lindsay's pony perform wonderful stunts in the riding arena. They were even happier to see her pony win a yellow ribbon for his well-executed fence jump. When it was all over, everyone prepared to leave.

Lindsay and her two new friends got to ride in the truck with her mother and father, while Winston's car was hauled in the horse trailer with Lindsay's pony. The ride through the country to Massachusetts in the late afternoon was restful and beautiful, as they traveled the long roads chatting happily. At one point, the three of them broke into song with their own version of "Old MacDonald's Farm," while Lindsay's parents stifled back their laughter from the front seats.

Much later that day, they reached Town's End and pulled into Lindsay's driveway. The White's house was a large cream-colored Victorian farmhouse with a flower garden in the front, and a barn in the back.

From an apple tree by the side of the house, hung a small-sized rope swing, which Lindsay's father had put up just for her.

Mrs. White cooked them all a late supper of stewed vegetable casserole and corn-on-the-cob. Then, Melody and Winston were shown the guestroom on the first floor where the three of them could sleep in sleeping bags on the floor like campers. They took turns preparing to wash up for bed and brushing their teeth (Melody, her bill) in Lindsay's made-for-her bathroom.

The next morning, Mrs. White called them for a delicious breakfast of popovers with powdered sugar sprinkled on top, and peppermint tea. She found some

dried sunflower seeds left over from last year's garden, which she gave to Melody.

Lindsay could not wait to show Melody and Winston around town. "Maybe I could find my old raft," said Lindsay excitedly.

"You have a raft?" asked Winston with a tinge of excitement.

"Yes, and there it is . . . at the river's edge!" shouted Lindsay.

"But . . . from what I can see, it looks rather damaged," replied Winston.

"Oh, don't worry—my father can fix anything," said Lindsay proudly. "I'll bet he could have that raft ready for sailing in no time!"

Lindsay was right. Mr. White went with them down to the river's edge where they found the damaged raft still banked among the rushes. In the time it

took Lindsay and her mother to pack up a picnic lunch, Mr. White had the raft fixed, watertight, and ready to go—complete with a new pole.

Chapter 15

A DAY OF CELEBRATION

Lindsay climbed onto the back of the raft, Melody hopped on the front, and Winston took up the center position with the pole in his hands. This meant, of course, that he would be both the navigator and the captain of the "watercraft." Winston had to admit that he felt quite good about himself for being in control of the raft while in the company of two of the prettiest females anyone could ever know.

They had a wonderful afternoon meandering down the smooth, flowing river. Lindsay gracefully dipped her hand over the surface of the water, making long ripples behind them, as Winston skillfully used the pole to push them along. Melody broke into a lovely tune of whistles that sounded as beautiful as the water itself.

When hunger finally had gotten to them, they sailed back up the river to a place they had spotted earlier for a picnic. Pulling the raft onto the sandbar, they climbed ashore the small island and ate their lunch. It was a marvelous day.

Mr. White was waiting for them at the river's edge when they returned.

"Wanted to make certain that you three would make it back—didn't want you to take off on us!" he said, smiling.

"Oh, Daddy, we wouldn't do that!" said Lindsay.

Suddenly, Winston began to feel a bit guilty. He wondered how Mr. Scott felt about him since he left home—especially since he and Melody had not reported a single story back to him.

Once back at Lindsay's house, Winston politely asked Mrs. White if he might be able to make a long-distance phone call to Brownsville, Maine.

"Why, of course, dear," replied Mrs. White.

"Getting a little homesick, Winston?" asked Mr. White.

"Well, it's just that it's been a long time since I've been home, and I don't know how much longer it will take to get back there from here," said Winston, suddenly feeling down in his spirits.

"I've got the perfect solution to your problem," said Mr. White. "Why don't we make a call suggesting that we put you both on the train for Portland, Maine? It would save you a lot of time, and you could be sure to arrive home safely."

"What a great idea, Daddy!" exclaimed Lindsay, jumping up and down.

"But, what about my car?" thought Winston aloud.

"You could leave it here so we could mail it to you, or I could package it up for the luggage car of the train," answered Mr. White.

"That would be great! Could I call Mr. Scott now, please?" asked Winston excitedly.

 Mrs. White dialed the operator and got through to Mr. Scott. After explaining who she was and her main reason for calling, Mrs. White put Winston up to the receiver to talk. Then, Mr. White got on the phone to work out all the details of the trip.

"I'd be putting them on the train in Boston, on the

morning run, probably arriving sometime around noon at the train station in Portland. I'll check the train schedule and call you back. . . . Um, hm. . . . Oh, no, don't worry about the train fare, as I have a feeling it will scarcely cost a thing for these two special passengers," said Mr. White as he smiled into the phone receiver.

The trip plans at last complete, the White family and their guests sat down to a *celebration supper*, as Winston named it.

"Not only are we here to celebrate the success of our upcoming trip home," said Winston, raising his water glass in a toast, "but, we are gathered together to celebrate our friendship and your wonderful family, Lindsay."

Mrs. White wiped a tear from her eye with her napkin as they all shouted, "Hear! Hear!" then tapped their glasses together.

The next morning, they all got up early for the trip into Boston. Mr. White drove his luxury sedan because, as he put it, "This is a special occasion, taking our adventurous guests to the train station!"

The three friends sat in the back on the fine leather cushioned seats. Mr. and Mrs. White, sitting up front, pretended to be their chauffeur and maid. Lindsay and Winston put on English accents in an attempt to sound *royal*. Melody assumed the airs of a movie star celebrity.

Coming into Boston, Winston was surprised how much it reminded him of what he had seen on his travels to Portland. Now, he really could not wait to get home.

Mr. White got them their tickets, which read, "Free ride for children under the age of six." He handed them directly to the conductor at the train, so that Winston and Melody would not be embarrassed about the reference to children.

After exchanging hugs and thank-yous, Mr. White lifted them aboard the train. Winston and Melody got another lift onto their seats by the conductor, then climbed up to the train's window ledge so they could wave goodbye one more time to Lindsay, and Mr. and Mrs. White.

As the conductor called out, "All aboard!" the train gave a jerk, and they were off! Winston and Melody hoped that their friend Lindsay would keep her promise to visit them in Brownsville someday soon.

Chapter 13

THE TRAIN RIDE

The scenery from Boston to Portland was fascinating. It reminded Winston of the ladies' quilts at the church auction—so many different colors and patterns woven together. He could barely keep himself awake with the lulling sounds of the train's movements, but he so wanted to see it all. The next thing he knew, the conductor was leaning over, tucking a small blanket around him and Melody.

"Lunch will be coming up shortly," whispered the conductor to Melody. "Will you wish to eat in the dining car, or would you prefer it delivered to your seat?"

"Here would be awfully nice, thank you," Melody whispered back.

"I'll be back with the menu shortly," continued the conductor. "Our next stop will be Portsmouth, New Hampshire."

By then, Winston was wide-awake. *Imagine going all this far in such a short amount of time*, thought Winston. *This is the way to travel*!

For lunch, Winston ordered a grilled cheese sandwich with a cup of hot chocolate. Melody chose the three-berry cobbler with a side order of sesame seed crackers. They arrived on silver trays with linen napkins and a thimble vase with tiny flowers.

After they finished their delicious lunch, the conductor came by with steamy hot cloths to wipe off any sticky remains of their meal. Winston and Melody were appreciating feeling like royal celebrities again, just as the conductor arrived with some coloring books and crayons.

"What's this?" asked Winston of the conductor.

"We like to give out these little train books to the children on the trip to keep them busy," replied the conductor.

Winston was not too certain how to take that remark, but he accepted the book and crayons anyway. The book had some interesting pictures of places of travel that intrigued him. The crayons might come in handy as a present for Duncan when he got home. Melody said that Winston could have her crayons as well, but that she would like to keep the book for a while, as it would remind her of their wonderful trip together.

Chapter 17

JOURNEY'S END

The rest of the way on the train to Portland went by rather quickly. When Winston finally got tired of hopping up and down from the window ledge to look at the scenery, he became content to rest in his comfortable seat. The conductor had stopped by with a pillow for him and Melody to share. It felt so good to relax in such luxury, that he almost fell asleep. But then, he might be arriving in Portland at any moment, and he certainly did not want to miss his stop!

Melody had to ask Winston to stop twitching in his seat because it was making the pillow move around and disturbing her. However, now, Winston had a reason to become excited because he began to see the skyline of Portland pass by his window. He was home!

The train pulled into Union Station as the conductor called out, "Portland, Maine!" Winston was about to hop up to the window ledge again, in hopes of seeing Mr. Scott on the platform outside, when he missed, becoming wedged between the seat and the window ledge.

Melody whistled for the conductor, who gently pried Winston out of his spot. "Best stay right here in your seat, young fellow," said the conductor. "I'll make sure the one who is picking you up comes into the train to get you both after the rest of the passengers depart." Winston wanted desperately to look for Mr. Scott himself, but Melody convinced him to wait.

As the various people cleared out of the train, there, coming down the aisle, was not only Mr. Scott, but Mrs. Scott and Duncan, as well!

"Winston!" they called. "You made it! You're back!"

"I can't believe it!" cried Mr. Scott. "And, you,

Melody, how are you doing?"

"You both are famous!" cried Duncan. "The news photographers are all over the station waiting to get pictures of you both! You're already in all the newspapers everywhere," he shouted with much enthusiasm.

After moving through all the crowds of photographers and reporters, they finally managed to get to Mr. Scott's car in the parking lot. This had been a never-before-dreamed-of-welcome-back gathering, but all Winston and Melody could think of now was how good it would be to return to their peaceful and beautiful hometown of Brownsville.

Chapter 18

WELCOME HOME.

When the two travelers arrived back at the Scotts' barn, there were quite a few surprises awaiting them. Mr. Scott had placed Winston's crate high on a shelf above his desk with an attached rope so he could swing down to the desk from above. This would keep him off the drafty barn floor and prevent any stray barn cat from getting to Winston.

Duncan had come over to help, as well, by cutting out a couple of small windows from the crate with his new carving knife he received for his birthday. Together, he and Mr. Scott had made a special roost with a perch for Melody on another shelf just above the one for Winston.

Mrs. Scott had cut out a felt rug for Winston's floor, added a few pieces of dollhouse furniture she had found in her attic chest from her childhood, and made a soft nesting pillow for Melody out of cotton stuffing and a piece of flannel she had in her sewing basket.

Winston and Melody were delighted with everything they saw, and could scarcely wait to try out their new homes in the barn. However, before they got too comfortable checking out their wonderful accommodations, Mrs. Scott called everyone to the table for a special supper. There were platters of macaroni in cheese sauce, steamy sweet potatoes, cheese-stuffed mushrooms, cornbread, and, for dessert, an apple pie made from the apples that were freshly picked from Mr. Flaherty's orchard. Mrs. Scott had made Melody's favorite muffin with birdseed on top, in her honor.

This time, Melody wanted to make a toast, which she sang out in trills, "To the best of friends a bird could ever have, to exciting journeys, and to welcome home parties!"

That evening, there was so much to tell each other that nobody wanted to go to bed. When they finally headed off to their new homes in the barn and drifted off to sleep in their comfortable beds, Winston and Melody were already dreaming of new and exciting places to explore on their next adventure together.

Author's Biography

A current resident of Higgins Beach in Scarborough, Maine, Joan Scott Candelmo was born and raised in Delaware. During her youth, she and her parents spent many memorable summers in Maine. Years later, she graduated from Bates College in Lewiston, Maine, where she first met and later married her husband, Philip. Over the years, she has been both mother and grandmother to her family, a kindergarten teacher in Bloomfield, Connecticut, a junior high Spanish teacher in Portland, Maine, and a specialized instructor to children with learning disabilities in Scarborough, Maine. During the most recent years, she and her husband were the owners of two retail stores, which operated for more than a dozen years in the Maine Mall.

Although she has written and illustrated several children's books of varied topics, her favorite character, E. B. White's *Stuart Little*, has been an inspiration to this latest story. Ever since her father began reading this most enjoyable adventure to her as a child, she has carried Stuart's spirit with her in her own style of storytelling. Readers will note there is something of Stuart's personality in the essence of *Winston Whitten*, which can be seen in her writings and in her pen and ink illustrations. The author sees this as her way of expressing her admiration for the esteemed writer, E. B. White, as well as the much-regarded illustrator, Garth Williams.

She loves collecting and sharing children's books with others, reading to young children in the classrooms, and hearing from those who also appreciate the magic of storybooks.

Ordering Information

In addition to several bookstores, copies of *The Far and Wide Travels of Winston Whitten* may be purchased by contacting:

Fiddlehead Publishing
8 Higgins Creek Road
Scarborough, Maine 04074

To order autographed copies and to obtain information about speaking schedules, please contact the author at:

Email: philjo@att.net

The cost of each book is $10.00, which includes shipping and handling.